MAYA

To Grace and Emma—M.J.

To all children and
those who love them—E.M.

Maya

Written by **Mahak Jain**

Illustrated by **Elly MacKay**

Owlkids Books

When the lights flickered,
Maya held her breath.
Then the electricity went out, for
the third time that week.

Mumma pumped the generator—
chugga—chugga—chugga. But it
was no use.

When Papa was alive, he would
light all the candles for Maya.
She would count the flames until
she fell asleep.

But candles didn't help anymore.
Now it felt as if the dark would
never go away.

Maya's mother pulled out a cot from storage and carried it to the roof. She lit two oil lamps.

"I wish Papa were here," Maya said.

Mumma hugged her. "Let me tell you a story."

Papa used to tell stories, too. He said that a story was like a bird. It flew you to places you had never heard of, and the places always changed you.

"The first monsoon was a long, long time ago," Mumma said. "The earth filled with rivers, and water seeped into the ground. Everyone was scared that the heavy rain would wash away their homes and destroy their crops.

"One little girl was especially afraid. What if the waters washed her away while she slept?"

Maya clasped her mother's hand. "This doesn't sound like a happy story."

"By the bank of a new river," Mumma continued, "rested a banyan tree. Just a sapling, it drank and drank and drank. The monsoon rains flowed through its roots. They fed its thirsty leaves and swelled its young trunk, and soon the sapling was a small tree.

"As the tree grew, so did the branches. They grew wider, until they could bear the weight of a tiger. They grew longer, until a peacock could strut in their shade. And then the branches sprouted roots that dropped like ropes, until a monkey could swing through them in play."

As Maya's mother spoke, the tree branches shook like a monkey was swinging through them. Was the pigeon on the balcony prancing like the peacock? And the autorickshaw growling past...

"It's a tiger!" Maya said.

Mumma smiled. "The roots sank into the earth and thickened into many trunks, until a snake could slink around unseen and an elephant could hide behind them. Soon, the tree had drained the flood. And so, the first banyan tree saved us from the first monsoon. No one was scared anymore. Not even the little girl."

Maya released her mother's hand. "The end?" she asked.

"The end," Mumma said.

The dark deepened and the city became quieter. Mumma fell asleep, but Maya still could not.

She started thinking about
the banyan tree from the story.
A tree so tall, she wouldn't be able
to see the sky through its leaves.
A tree so wide, she wouldn't be
able to see what was on the other
side. If Maya walked between the
banyan tree's many trunks, it
would be dark, even if the sun
outside shone.

Maya grasped Mumma's hand—
but her mother did not wake.

Maya lifted her head. She heard the snake hissing, ready to strike. She sensed the tiger sneaking, searching for prey.

She sat up. The monkeys above cackled and broke branches. The peacock attacked the tree with its beak. And the elephant crushed everything under its heavy step.

Maya's heart thudded and she felt light-headed from fear. She covered her eyes, and then she remembered her mother's story. It had been scary at first, but by the end the story was wonderful.

Maya thought about the hissing snake as she climbed one of the banyan's trunks. She peered down and saw that the snake was not hissing. It was rustling the leaves as it slithered to and fro.

Maya thought and thought some more. She jumped down to another trunk and peeked through a clump of hanging roots. She saw that the tiger was not sneaking. It was rubbing its soft fur to ease an itch.

As the branches above shook, leaves rained down. Light peeked through. And Maya saw that the monkeys were not cackling... they were laughing as they played.

The peacock was not striking its beak...it was feeding on seeds.

And the elephant was not crushing everything in its path...

...it was dancing.

Maya dropped down and walked into the center of the tree, where only shadows danced. It was dark, but she thought of her father. She thought of him whistling while walking her to school.

She closed her eyes and heard his familiar tune. And the fear she felt floated away.

Maya was tired. Her arms were weak from climbing and her legs were sore from jumping. Even the animals began to slow. They stopped what they were doing and started to doze. She followed the sound of her mother's gentle snores and returned to the roof.

Mumma opened her eyes. "You're still awake?"

"I couldn't sleep," Maya said.

Her mother began to hum Papa's lullaby. Maya's eyes drooped. Even though she could not see him, she knew Papa was not far away. As she fell asleep, she sensed him, tucked inside her mind.